JellyMan's Collection of Peotics*

This time it's personal

Jeff Fountain

Jeff-Fountain.net

***Peotics.** Noun: (arcane usage) Of literature; compositions of poor poetry, written in the vain hope that someday someone will read it.

Also by Jeff Fountain

Like a James Dean Cigarette
A novel
Even Continents Drift
Short Stories
Croydon Beach
Short Stories

Published by Jeff fountain at Amazon

Please note that there are very occasional uses of language that may cause offence.

Cover Art: **FlapCat Design**

Dedication

MB

Contents

A man is running

It's your age she said.
Yes, my rage he said
deliberately misunderstanding her

And so, a man is running,
running across a field.
Shortening the distance to where he is going
Lengthening the distance of where he has been
He looks ahead fearful
of what he might find
Fearful of what he left behind
His stride is steady and it is strong
But as with all things,
it will be so for long

It will slow it will fade
Tired at the chase
his story scribed into his face
And in the ache of age
he will turn to face
His tormentors and his fate

Punished by gods and minor deities
With all the gifts that on him showered
Angry they vent their ire
Upon him
For a life not led
But casually shed

Run from a life in between
He is cursed to run out his term
vanquished by his own timidly

Sounds scream in his head
A high pitched Why-ne
With all that you had
You let go so cheaply

15th December 2009

The shore untied

Let loose the boats
and float them free
I am the shore untied.

You are my heart untied.
Are you my heart untied.

Unreeve the sails
cast off the chains
I am the shore untied
You are my life untied.

Haul up the anchor
now pull on the oar
I am the untied shore
You are my love untied.

Open the ocean
full and wide
Fill up the sky with stars
Mine is the freed uncaptive soul
You are my unfettered bride

Sail that tender tide
Make for that land
Where you are
You are my centre
You are my I

Who is the flood?
Who the tide
where is the tiller
where is my guide

I have done with the sea
Done with its treachery
Done with drowning waves
Done with its sirens
Done with its graves

You are my love restored
You are my heart repaired
To be home to be home
once more
tied safe to that shore

You are my shore
You are my home
You are my heart
you are my heart's second beat

22nd February 2017

La campagne française

Outside is cold and sunny
The dirt needs digging
And weeds need pulling
The farmer wants money
Always wants money

The hares are running
escaping the jug
The deers darting
from venison destiny
They are out there
Out there gunning
Them down for sport – for sport
... for sport

Worms are turning
Slowly into fledglings
Tunnelling moles
Shot whilst trying to escape
Gentile Rabbis scamp homeward
Missing their T

Hedgehogs bristle
And prick the air
Lizards warm and taste that air
Echoes of geckos
Even Icarus turns his back on the sun
To get an even tan

But it's the sun that gets even

The farmer whiskers in his den
Plotting the fall of kings

28th March 2017

Resurrection Road

A man
(of indeterminate age)
pulls on his hat
then on his cigarette
and steps into the rain

Every drop misses him
despite the deluge

That's lucky
he says
walking along
And removing his hat

The falling safe hits him
- square and ironically
but resurrection is
just a frame away
in Cartoon Street

Why are they called safe
He wonders
as a thousand pianos wait
in the heavy clouds

29th March 2017

An Old Friend Visits

Why have you called me back?
Asks my old friend
in my sleep

Why are you in my sleep I ask
and we talk
She is as I remember

We didn't agree
Did she leave her sleep to join me?
Does she ever?

Let's give it another go
I say
Fuck off she says
Not feeling vulnerable and naked
But she was naked.

I must miss her
I didn't tell her
To come back again
Soon
Before it's too late

31st March 2017

Quantum Mechanics and Me

All countries are great
They say
Each one better
than all the rest
Yet Quantum Mechanics
says
That an atom cannot exist in the
same place as another...

God is great
There is only one God
And he is fab
But it seems
Everybody has a different
One
And all theirs are the fabbest too
Yet Quantum Mechanics says...

There are many planets
But we can only live on this
One
So we behave
as if... y'know
Yet Quantum Mechanics says...

There is only one me
And I am great
I am individual

But everybody
is a me
Yet quantum theory says...

You have only one life
So live It
Yet we watch TV and wait
for life to turn up

Quantum Mechanics doesn't care
about this
Or you
Or god
Or your country
Or your life

6th April 2017

Between Things

I fit
In between
things
Between religions' bias

I fit
between
colours of
dark and daring

I fit
in between
states
Death and dying

I fit
between
My birth and living

I fit
between
Longing and life

I fit
between
Me and you

I fit
in the middle
of my hue and the eyes of others

I fit
in between the bark and howl
between dog and wolf
Between us and others
strangers and lovers
Between the oil can and a squeal
The road and the wheel
Disease and shame
sleep and pain

between all the ands
that ever there were and will be

Because of this
I fit as the outcast fits
into Eden's banishment
Naked save for you.

6th April 2017

Phosphate of Calcium

Phosphate of Calcium
Is bone
they tell me
But I don't believe
a word
I am held up
by will alone
and not by common bone

The heart is a pump
They trump
But I say no
It is the organ of love
and woe

The brain
I read
is the body's processor
the central control
But I insist
I exist
by spirit and by soul

If all living nature
is accident
where Darwin's chemistry set's
to survive intersects
How is it then
That I feel so fucking alive

11 April 2017

The Invention of cancer

Yes you do have cancer
Said the jellyman
No, he replied
It has me

He held his hand
To shake
But it shook
All by itself

Your cells are now
The centre of your world
Your world is now
A cell

He promises
An ode to each
New sun
A contemplation
To be wished for devoutly.

13th April 2017

After Dinner

I come home
Make soup
With bread
Then I watch
TV
After I go to bed
And I
Dream

Each night he returns
To the well
And wheels the bucket high
Drinking deeply
Enthusiastically
Slaking his thirsty
desires.
But this night
This night of all
His nights
It will be dry

His dry dreams
emptied of
Youth's empire

He is found
Inconsolable
Above cold soup

his bread stale
In front of his TV
As the dreams flicker on

13th April 2017

32 Cramp Street

Squeezed into a brick suit
that no longer fits
The man dares to
expand his desires
beyond his confinement

Jammed between the jabbering jaws
of neighing neighbours
like a tethered balloon
his fancy floats
to get beyond it all.

Screwing eyes press
into his quiet fancies
and bellying over every one
mush them
to mere laughter
and ridicule

Now from under this mountain …
he cuts his imagination
free.
'Scapes the crushing burden from
all sides
And hovering above for one more
moment
lifts
oh so

gently
drifts leaf-like
breezeward
into a cloudless yonder
and
is
        gone

17th April 2017

Sleep-less

the twin of death
if this is what death is like
we can believe in ghosts
that never quite rest

for I heard voice cry out
sleep no more!
MacJeff hath murdered sleep

18th April 2017

Why you should never believe your Parents

They said I was beautiful
   I wasn't
They said I was clever
   Eye yam knot
Said I wouldn't grow
   I did
They said they'd be proud
   There were – but not of me
Said I would be confident
   And I squirm
They said I would make a great father
   I am no farther on
They told me I would be handsome
   I became a tory
Would be a complete success
   I just got to succ
Be a grateful son
   I tried
That I would help them
when they grew old
   they grew old in spite of me.
They said I would be content
          But I miss their words

22nd April 2017

Please Knock

This is the house that Jeff Built
Here is the door
That Jeff scoured
Please knock

This is the room that Jeff built
Here is the window
that Jeff blinded
Please knock

This is the garden that Jeff made
Here is the gate
That Jeff made – hung
Please knock

Here is the life that Jeff spent
Blinded
Scoured
Made and Hung
Please knock

27th April 2017

Cramp Street Blues

Well I wakes ever' mo'nin'
To the sound of brats a'bawlin'
As they pass by my window
Each day comes a'dawnin'

Cramp Street, oh, cramped street
Where I'm aching and beat
Between the grinder and the meat

They hallelujah and cry
Then squawk and sigh
I hate school, hate school
I'll hate learnin' till ah die

Cramp Street' oh, cramped street
Where I'm aching and beat
Between the match and its heat

The cars come a'rattlin'
Down Cramp Street battlin'
To find a place to rest fo'
The night's TeaV'in'

Cramp Street, oh, cramped street
Where I'm aching and beat
Between the knife and the bleat

They creep, poke and squint
For the smallest hint
In windows for a life
with some inkling or glint

Cramp Street, oh, cramped street
Where I'm aching and beat
Between the sickle and the wheat

Oh, I long to leave
Long to leave
The Street with with no shame
This Street without shame

Cramp Street, oh, cramped street
Where I'm aching and beat
Between the grinder and the meat

2nd May 2017

Art

I am full of art's intentions
Lacked by invention
I wander the picture halls of the sublime
Framed and hung by my own pretensions

4th May 2017

Wealth

A man of limited means
Is walking in the woods
And finds a discarded pair of boots
They are old and careworn
The laces slippery from rain
Inside mould grows

He looks at the soles
and they are sound
The stitching of the uppers
Holding – fast
The only shine is the one
they have for the old man

He looks at his own boots
About the same size
Yes, try them
He eases his feet from their fetid enclosure
And slips them easily
into the found pair.
Perfect – the glove of boots
he smiles

He considers his old boots
They have been with him many years
and many miles
It feels like betrayal
Not-withstanding

he leaves them
in the place he found his new ones
and goes his way
….

A man of limited means
Is walking in the woods
And finds a discarded pair of boots
They are old and careworn
The laces slippery from rain
Inside mould grows.

10th May 2017

Jelly Man 2

NO! It does not have me
I have it
This is my disease
I own it now
He smiled to the Jelly Man

It will kill you
He wobbled and shook
It will not
I will kill me

How long have I have got
to live?
Oh, we cannot say, cannot tell
So, which is it?
Tell or say?

So, how long have I got to live?
I do not know.
No one has to live

He shivered on his chair
liquefaction imminent
aren't you going to cry?
You must know you are going to die

He watched close
through melting eyes

Ok, how long must I live?
For as long as you can
Dissolve – his jelly paunch
running from his shirt

Now is the time to cry
as he began to liquify
No, it is not
you go cry for me
and humanity
- he was done

I am just doing my job
he said spreading at my feet
Then do it better
do it for us !

I stepped from the room
Sloughing off the jelly
he closed the door
And went to confront
HIS destiny

11th May 2017

Milton's Road Lost

Gone now
Milton's lost road
West of Hendon
No Paradise lost, no.
Fog gotten in history's mist

But look, look!
Through the blear,
There, there I am,
young
too young to care
I am peddle car 6 and six
but lower in the grand of things

Waking up as from a long sleep
I watch as my feet walk
my hands reach
My body works
like trying on a new suit

Tarry initials laid out
on the curb
that sweat and run
to the gutter
Identity begins and the child is lost

Dad bigger than the house
gives all for us
Mum smarter than wise

mumbles in a foreign tongue
Understands much

School coat hook
hung my plimsol bag
dinner money bag
(5 Shillings)
like an early tie
sewn by her

I can feel the love
poured over me like it's
Lyles' syrup
sticky-sweet
and solid I can almost eat

Teachers in welsh
thigh slapping angry
for some reason
whisper in a different foreign tongue
Told to hush
not to brazen
ask for
go for
want more
- or any, or any save
be content
then Number 6 peddles
me bumping down Milton's Road

Go back to where you came from!

They will shout

Oh, if I could I would
Back to then
when streets were kinder
and hearts beat slower
and the apple still hung in its place

13th May 2017

Summer – Flight 2017 is ready to board

Are you new season cushion ready
Are you beach bag ready
Are you skin care ready
Are you worth it ready
Are you bikini ready
Are you abs ready
Are Vagina ready
Are you cocksure ready
Are you life ready
Are you anything ready
Are you ready for anything ready
Are you happy ready
Are you ready for take off ready
Are you ready – for anything
?
Ready? – Really, ready?

How can you be so sure?

6th July 2107

The Invention of Clothes

(Falling)

When Adam at first woke
Stretched and yawned
and carefree, gazed about
and took his first piss
did he then look down
to shake it out – wondering...
was he circumcised?
Why did he have balls?
when he stood proud
did he wonder out loud?

And Eve before her curse
did she fare much worse?
I am different from you
said Eve pointing
You have what I have not
They must get in the way a lot

They talked of nothing
just watched
just grunted
at the animals and trees
to the fish in the seas
at the birds in the air
then lay back, naked and bare
as god had intended

Day after day
with nothing to do
but wander and chew
the goodness that grew
all around them in feasts
then thought
is this all there is?
Is there nothing but this?

And then a teacher
(cursed be that name)
that low bellied creature
unnerving them 'gainst almighty wrath
said, "These are good questions
come see what can be done
with fruit and some fun."

(Fallen)

Now recognising the 1
and then the O
that one fits the other
like so and like so
they tried each other for size
and were a pretty good fit
and realised
they were naked
and fig-ured some clothes

Then through his garden a'walking
God came a'calling

to see how His favourite creations
were doing
saw them bedecked and festooned
with flowers and broom

They shrank away lest
He ask them to divest
what *they* had created
whilst He was at rest
Oh, no not you!
You were the best thing
I've done
now you'd better run
Close the gates behind
and never look back

So, outside they stood
abandoned, without food
the wilderness beckoned
now what would they do?
but the 1 and the O
had a strange draw
and off came their clothes
and together they came
together they rolled
at the groin
were conjoined
and for a moment at least
it was heaven
it was lost eden's naked bliss.

7-8th July 2017

The Daystone

I walked upon a summer grass
And into a small wood
The air became still upon entering

And there, under a small shrub
found a gravestone worn with rain
aged by wind
grown old and
Overgroan under it's granite weight.

A name, if there had been one
was long disappeared as I imagined
the body that once lay below
just the rock and date remained
1st October 1817

Was this, the day
the day that had died? merely
that lay beneath had been
not a man
or woman
just time buried and marked,
passing through the
brief year.

Behind me the sun
was declining
as I turned to greet
the closing hour

8th July 2107

The things that divide

There's you, vous and du
Sound familiar?

And me, moi and mir
Again?

Of course there's us, nous and uns
All have us in them, right?

So, what's the problem, probleme, problem?

21st July 2017

Waiting for a connection

Waiting for a connection
Says my speaker
Married tomorrow
says my diary

Top up
says my phone
Be good
says my brain

Ready for the workout start
says my apple
Help me
Says my heart

Don't worry
says a missed call
worry
says my tiny voice

Eat now
says my stomach
don't eat
says my front paunch

Eat me
says my pie
Don't you dare
says my conscience

Get up
says my clock
why
says my pension

Listen
says a friend
I will
I say, drifting somewhere

28th July 2017

The Elephant Driver of Nantes

Hello dear
How was your day?
Asks the driver's wife

Alors – normalement.
He replies tiredly
Staring passed his repast
to his first love
Normalement ma chère
Giving way to
Let a yawn through

Tell me about it,
I'll understand?
She urges him
Across the crudités and
Slicing sensitively
through his pain

I drive my elephant
At ten hours a mile
Eight hours a day
Trumpeting our way
through laughing happy people
drenching joyful children
With my mechanical trunk
Quelquesfois it feels
Like it drives me

When he yawns
and sighs
It sounds like an
elephant

You look très très
fatigué
Is the work
That hard mon chère?

No, mon amour
it is wonderful
It's my smiling
That wears me out.

1st August 2017

Upon greeting

Hey, what gives?
Nothing much.
I find
It just takes

A long while ago

Sine Qua Non

Where there is life
there be hope,
and where be hope
there is life

...They say

But what if,
if all hope is extinguished
all hope realised
all hope abandoned
all of it denied
for those
who enter this life?
then surely without hope
therc is no life.

No plan
no future imagined
no resurrection
no cure
no bigger house
better car
no children
no mercy
no justice
no human desire
for anything

But now
Imagine
for just a moment
a solitary moment
one fragment of time
and then with each moment
laid end upon end
a sequence of moments

imagine

What freedom truly is... hopeless

12th August 2017

An english airman sees another fate

(Apologies WBY)

There is something,
Thought the young pilot
Flying eastward,
Something about the man
Earthbound, waving
His manner
His stature
Something
familiar.

He throttled back briefly
and, dipping his wings
in dumb salute
turned lazily home
for Kiltartan Cross

A man stands
a hand
above his head
Is he shading his eyes
As he looks to the skies?
Or caught in the middle
Of waving?
Is he troubled?

The plane is now
Too far away
yet

he waves
Once more
but with less
enthusiasm
realising
at what he waves
disappeared
a long time before
along with his longing

His arm sinks
To his side
His head falls
eyes fixed
solemnly
on the rooted ground

he recedes
Way back
To when he dreamed
of wings
but now he
is just another Icarus
Unwaxed
Unfeathered
With the sun waiting
still
Waiting
for him

14th August 2017

The girl who passed me by – 1nce

I recall her
Long hair
Combed out
like a wedding train
that face
almost divine
in a young man's eyes

Her look at
Me – me
That look that so
Beguiled and taunted
And
Haunted me since

Just too shy
to say hi,
Hello as I work
The car outside
Hi I would say
And she would
Say hi and it
Might have begun

But no
I just glanced back
Saying nothing
But driving my

Longing want deep
down into my coyness

I never knew
Her
Name
What number
She lived at
Floating by
In slo-mo
Sublime
I think I was
In love
Then

Now I am
Wintered in age
And disease.
I know there
Is no going around
again
What might have been
But to imagine
A different passing
When she would
Stop
And ask my name

27th August 2017

A cigarette's embrace – 2wice

There
Right there
On that bus
She sat next me
And offered a smoke
A light in my life
That could have
Burned all the way
Through my torment
No thanks
I had said
And in silence
And
For thirty seven years
I wondered
About that smoke
Denied
drifted away
Another beauty
Passed me by

You fool
You had fortune
And looks
But no courage
No
Courage

28th August 2017

A pigeon's courage – 3rice

Two pigeons
one dipping and nodding
at the other bemused
a late summer courtship
she watches
he tries
and tries again
but she flies
he looks surprised
at least he tried
a failed coo d'coeur
but
a pigeon's fancy
greater than mine

29th August 2017

Pride

She stood
in imperious beauty
self conscious
aloof
proud of her
breasts
for indeed
they stood
proud
of her

2nd September 2017

Just deserts

There is something
about sand
something about that
land
wherein it drifts
that lifts
the spirit
where man's hand
is absent
and that
absence, that lack
is called
desert -
just that
and nothing
more

3rd September 2017

To be or not to

witch
friend
knownst
lie
calmed
nighted
fuddle
labour
lay
smirch
fuddle
deck
fall
draggle
moan
hold
little
devil
grudge
loved
sotted
reave
twixt
gambleaware
drinkaware
rexit

fucked

4th September 2017

Walk from the room laughing

if my life were a space
it would be a room
large and boundless
but a room
n'er the less

In my room
I would unorder
things unclutter them
dispense all the noise that
silent
things make
demanding your consideration.

no shelves
of nick-nacks
screaming to be noticed
no ornaments
crying for attention
no statuettes eyes filling
with dust tears
sans silent sea-side souvenir shells
she sold 'side some
sandy seashore

In that room
each day there
I would stretch
and nothing touch

in compass round
save the air walls
and ceiling sky
clear
and free
all the way to
heaven's reach

5th September 2017

On Reflection

Was it the jealousy's rage
or the mirror's tongue
That cursed and
mantled beauty
in sleep for 100 years?

There in that
glass she can see
her mother
shining back at her
craggied with age
no more
but with soft wishes
and a smile
that would bring seven years
misfortune
should it wish to
but no
she looks and sees
a century's
blessing

Beauty slumbers on
ageless but unaware
and dreams of
wakeless sleep

16th September 2017

The hare doesn't run any more
- All bets are off

They don't bet at Hackney any more
The dogs are silent
the hare put away
museumed in some cupboard
now moth chased going mad
Saturday's hunting parody
for gamblers; the luckless
and now, for them
The hare does not run any more

They don't bet in Mecca bookies anymore
King's Cross' smokey Kabbalah
standing room only
men in carpet slippers tiptoe round
to Haj from tiny houses
and stand like greyhounds with their slips
clutched
20p each way in illiterate hands
straining upon the start
then in a breath's curse
Union Jacks flutter to the floor
Yankees go home
Accumulators blow
The call to prayer
silent but...

The hare doesn't run anymore
Mecca Bookmaker now a book seller
In that quiet press of pages
If you listen you can hear
The hare is running at Hackney
They bet Hackney
Photo Hackney
Result Hackney… trap...
The cursed luck
the shake and slide of small coins
crossing the counter
for the last race
But they don't bet at Mecca anymore.

There were six traps at Hackney
And one trap in Mecca -
maker of books
to the faithful
where losing bets
in hope momentarily dashed
scatter the floor
and licked pencils
are eased behind ears

They don't bet in Mecca anymore
The call to hare silent at Hackney
But somehow
In my head
It still runs
and keeps running
swift and sure

the hounds
tearing after it
like lost bets fluttering
as in real life
cross a field zig-zagging for life
it runs
and runs
and runs

4th November 2017

Bred and Dripping

Drip drip
my life drips away
a melting candle
no light
no heat
just the sizzle
of burning fat.

Yet I am cold
and in the dark
with thieves and robbers
all around.
I am grown to this
Become prisoner and gaoler
sinner and priest

11th November 2017

The remains of history (For Greg A)

Some people fall
through cracks
in time
unsung and unremembered
And in time
of course
everyone does
So, when trawling through
some gathered grime
happened upon
forgot till now
a small card – a lifetime

Memories of him flash
like teeth (I suppose) in my smile
recalling his small history
meanwhile
the card – with his name and nothing more
is slipped through a crack in the floor
to wait for some future
light
to find him once more

And beneath those same boards
scattered and hid
lie many of those things
I did
in a life like his
unmarked
passed by
as yet
largely
unlived

13th November 2017

Epigram in Stone
(and schmaltz)

I visited Bernie's stone today
that shelters him under.
In a small bay of stones
each with its name
each with a number

By that stone
I loosed a tear
(was it for me?)
And wished him well,
well
it was all I could do
'cept tell him – take care.

Sad, though it is
to converse with a stone
as if stone could hear
had flesh
as if it had bone
but it's all we have
for us now bereft
and alone

Let's remember then
and perhaps
alongside or
maybe nearby
my stone shall stand
and share that good company
of a well loved man.

14th November 2017

My Arse as a Kipper
– Father's Curse

I am listening to
comedy,
comedians
on the radio
and I cannot raise laugh
My arse is a kipper

Industrial strength comedy
'How is every one
Anyone here from somewhere
Take my wife'
Take a knife and
Take my life - please
But I cannot laugh
My arse is a kipper

rattling along the
production line
off they roll
all with a manufactured
fractured take
on life
The Jestapo have come for us
His dog has no nose
Her dog doesn't eat meat
but my life went to the west indies

Jamaica?
lucky thing

My arse *is* a kipper

I remember my father
arm-chaired
watching the TV
in case something happened
close and careful
like a guard to a precious jewel
watching
lest a joke pass him by
unguffawed, unchuckled,
but
no matter how hard he watched
nothing emerged
finally
'If,'
he said,
'if that man is a comedian
my arse is a kipper!'

I laughed
I cried
and shook
at that thought
my father's kippered arse

17th November 2017

Leave a message
(an everyday meeting with a genome sequencer)

He is not Available
Will you wait
    Not Available -
    How long has he been
    Not Available?
Some time now.
He became unAvailable
Some time ago now.

    Remind me -
    When was it
    he first became
    Available?
Don't know.
He always looked younger
Than his Availability date.
    Yes, that's true

    Can I leave
    a message?
If you like.
    Will he get it?
I doubt it.
    No point then?
Not really

I'll leave a message anyway.
OK.
What shall I say?
Up to you.
Tell him him
that I asked after him.
That's nice.
Thank you.
And that I am Available
for him any time OK?
Right

Feared of dying.
I'm sorry, what?
As he didn't do
Enough living
So really
He'd been unAvailable
All his Availability

22nd November 2017

Scene from a Train

Pulling out of Ladywell Station
There, as if blown by a breeze
I glimpse a handkerchief
A tiny garden
hugged about by
hunching houses
The winter plot
barely enough for a seat
and a slow worm's stroll.
The neat lines, close lawn,
shrubs tidy and snipped
to inch perfection.
Impatient bulbs
awaited their spring turn
in the crackling earth.
I imagine the garden
returning this love
to all the encircling eyes
that looked upon it
each day, every day.

A garden for all
Even for those heads down
London bound
if they care to see
care to look around

Yet out there not
thirty miles since
in the train's train
sits a singular house
aspect reversed
surrounded
by lolling gardens
that roll acre upon acre quiet
across the parkland
pasture and meadowsweet
and neighing paddocks
a kempt walled orangery
fallow now in winter's grip
The house shrunk by tamed nature
it is a garden
for one

Yet who would
bend to whisper
and ask that vast forgiving ground:
Are you as loved
as that little green yard
framed by people
a pictured scene?

14 December 2017

Now Here is NowHere

Stuck fast
on solstice day
stuck fast
as the season turns
I can watch
the days grow
and nights shrink
snowdrops squeeze
from winter's clamp

Frisk is in the air
the promise
of congress
The earth begins to flex
and small flecks
break to breath

Stuck fast
The man in change
the new Ducati – a gear change
his other mistress
The mother's first sweats
Young girls and their new breasts
boys stare – obsessed

Stuck fast
Earth sweeps it's clock
rounding the sun's dial
for an even tan

the darkest day
the longest night

All around
all nature
is on the move
I am here
and here becomes nowhere
Stuck fast
I am a watcher
a listener
impatient

21st December 2017

That look

Seconds
Perhaps fewer
That's all it took
That look

Passing
It pulled me in
A hook
That look

Wondering
What it could have held
Promising an old schnook
That look

Glancing
She and he
Young and beautiful
Ancient and crook
That look

30 December 2017

In the Aquarium

We are watching
Our ancestors swim
Watching us
take pictures
They
quietly take
Us in

2nd January 2018

The Pilot

There is a figure
hunched
Over the bed
Not threatening
Coated and calm
Large – he(?) sits
And watches
At the man's side

Does the man
Know he is there?
He smiles as if
He is happy
lost in some fond dream
As if he is about to float
Lift clear
Shake free
waiting
he stays locked
Quiet
In his cloudy reverie

The heavily coated man
In the warm June room
Is still
Still there
Unmoving
But moving
Something
In the man

Then he is gone
And by mourning
So is the man

23rd January 2018

Fond Obsequies for Enz O'lutimide*

This is the end
beautiful friend
the Enz
adieu capsule pal
you each cost more
than Gagarin's that day
you kept at bay
my rampant PSA
and did my life extend

Sorry Jeff
I did my best
for quite a while
but your PSA
was just too (bloody!) hostile

No, no,
say it ain't so
Enz O'
I'll miss your sweats
well, actually, no
- but only those.

Time for another mistress
for a different drug
another one's kisses
another one's hugs

Each day you called
you made me swallow
you shrank my balls
and bid me follow
And I did, I did it all

And now you are more girlie
a lot less burly
no so hairy
actually
a bit of a fairy
- tell me squarely
do they call you Mary?

It wasn't my fault
you had to go
I wanted you to stay
but the jellymen say no
the jellymen say go

But it was you to blame
you got in this game
if you'd seen the threat
we'd never have met

You're right
you're quite correct
I let myself down
I am the poisoned clown

Nice knowing you Jeff
but I gotta go

gotta depart
you'll find someone else
I know it's a blow
bit of a fart

So long, so long so
ma petite EnzO,
thanks for your help
but you never know
I could be here a while
to raise a smile
once in a while
when I remember
my carer, my lover – EnzO

24th January 2018

* Enzalutamide is a hormonal drug

Star in a Jar
(an organ's lament)

Somewhere
in some medicine
cabinet
wallows an organ
jarred and sliced
examined and
needled
filed and noted
studied
and prodded
- a tonsured star

it had served me well
creating
creative juices
to carry my mirrors
into the world
for sixty years
or so
and I was still using it
when it was wrenched
from me
distressed
diseased
and now deceased
(unAvailable)

it has done for me
that thing
and soon enough
for sure
but in that jar
under those lights
a stage is prepared
for 50 years hence

all that I produced
all that remains
not these lines
not these wishes
not my hoped fors
and desires
just
that small prostate notion
the thing that should give life
took mine
the cutter's knife missing it
by months
now, there it swims
in its smug formaldehyde
an ingenue
waiting for the call
waiting to tell my story
to those who care to know
to those who care

and so as it is pulled
from its jar
will they wonder
about its creator
the man who
gave *it* all that downunder
inner life
and now its own
showy afterlife

28th January 2018

The Unmaking

If I could
I would
return to all those
I harmed
and unharm them

Then at the event
of my death
like a settler's wagon
on an urban roundabout
surrounded
by machines
screaming for blood
firing exhausted
poison arrows
circling circling
honking for the kill
I'll wait
to cross over

then knowing I'll not make it
to The Otherside
I would leap
and take wing
strain against the pull
of earth's weight for
a thermal ride
high above the road
and it's grubby embrace

Then to find
I am light
as a single molecule of air
and so float up and up
away
away from sight

"Who was he – a bird, angel, aviator?"
Some might ask of
my other
"no, he used to be a dreamer
and in dreaming
crossed over."

7 February 2018

There's a hole in the future

There's a hole
in the future
there's a space
in time
Then – there's you
in your place
there's me
in mine

There's a void
and a tear
in what's to come
that cannot be filled
and cannot
be 'scaped from

Yet take heart
take cheer
forget time
enjoy now
have pleasure
in the moment
hold back the next chime

The future is history
just a bygone to come
cut adrift
illusion's boat
and watch it drift
make a gift of the present
and the present a gift

21st February 2018

Waiting for a train

There's a sign
Outside the town,
LaFleche it's called,
A sign that splits old rails

For me it holds a hope
Certainly forlorn
Of trains that will
Again move in and out
Like breath giving
Life back to the place

Yet despite this doubt
I still see it
A renewal of faith
For a time that connects
Everyone to everywhere
No matter their pocket
No matter their purse

This tiny sign
Is still there
Splitting old rails
That one day again
Would ring to that
Glorious sound

"The train arriving"

BRaiN Gun at the Window

I have a rifle
that can be trained
It has foresight
and can predict
someone's future
and hindsight
to see their past
in their passing

By its nature
it has no feelings
just indifferent intent
It can be hired
like any gun
and fired
like anyone

I have a rifle
of the highest calibre
it can aim
and point
and scope

in my hands it is
as light as a wage
and purposed
heavy as a rail

But it is jammed
in the breach
and I cannot reach
the place.
and as my targets pass
the window
my finger aches
my soul craves
for release.

Who would miss them?
I wouldn't.

17th April 2018

We have a guest

You wouldn't have guest
Not this one
Uninvited it flies in the face
of our hospitality
It takes an unhealthy interest
in our food
and menaces us
as we read.

It heads for the window
and heads the window
and heads the window
and heads
so on and on
he is tired of our company
and longs for the gulping embrace
of the fields of recent manure

I open a window
go
I say
but no
back into the room
He chooses death over freedom
Strange choice

My killing slipper waits
its chance
But though the fly
has a thousand eyes
even so
still it dies
- ephing flies.

12th May 2018

The Wish

So... A wish
that everlasting wish.
I have to return
to this place
like a pilot's return to earth.
Ineluctable
drawn to my state
of gravity
falling back
crashing wingless
and cramped
not as in a cockpit aloft
but like a corpse below
into its grave.

4th June 2018

Bye Plain Man

Cars stamp and crunch
upon the crumpled and ripple road
they roar and run
almost cursing the day with their grunts.
Rubber hisses and spits along
their cacophonous corridor
with each and every one
 - a warning
the deadly snake of the quotidian
we (must) dance macabre out their way
the filthy raptors of the living day

Then
two birds
chorus above the devil din
and I stretch up to hear their
songs crackle the air
Male and female perhaps
a right of fancy
beautiful to sightless eyes
they sigh above
a deep throbbing bubbling song
double winged the very
mock of dragon flies
steady in level flight
careless of the frothing
ordinariness of the below.

I wait and watch for them to disappear
and surely they do
sad to see them go
as back into my senses
roars that beast again.
And I am laid low
Chewing-gummed to Corrugation Street
I slouch my way
grounded
my head still in the air
a Johnny always head in air
always head in air

9 June 2018

The Preconceived Offer

If you could
You would
Perhaps ask
The permission
Before admission
Into this life

You would show
The things that you know
that might befall
Your infant
to a
Life yet born
yet even conceived

Here a lesson learned
There a heart that yearned
Someone's death
A deep remorse
an infidelity and
and passing hate
A consummation
All too brief a happy state
a catalogue through all the days
moon beams
and sun's rays

- This life

you will tell of your
burden to choose
another's life
not your own
as if by right
you chose alone

should you if you could tell all
the haps and stances
that *will* befall
their life chances
of their short time
and give them pause
and stay your offer
lest you be cursed and torn
by your child's bitter tongue
'I was not asked to be born!'

18 June 2018

Life Explained
(for MB)

How do you feel?
asked the kindly stranger
of the hapless man
        In conscience, answered he,
        I feel like death
        like I cease to be

But you hear that call,
asked the stranger,
That cry
of the buzzard high
as it skirts the skies
on unfolded wings
and shrieks of sheer delight?
        He listened and could hear
        only falling's deadly fear

Can you feel that breeze
soft against your skin
perfumed in the scent
of summer's bright
Blake's garden of sweet delight?
        He felt and could touch
        only bleak's bitter night

Can you not hear
the buzz and hum
of the land alight
with joy and life and light?
    He listened and was deaf to all
    save only fear and fright

Can you not see
your wife's smile
as she tends you (ur)gently
through her love
burdened by *your* woe?
    he tried to look but tears
    blurred her vision
    into misery's black crow

The stranger, in angel's
disguise, departing said,
then trust in your heart
for if it's death you feel
it has already ceased to beat
and fleeing upwards
left the man
to his demise
calling: Life without joy
is mere compromise.

21 June 2018

The Embezzler

Come along with us
you reprobate
you shrivelling Harpagon -
for company just your ledgers
your tally stick-
stack for consolation
buried by your treasures

You were in charge
of the counting room
left amongst the dusty volumes
between the unswept shelves
your whole life
high on your desk you sat
Scroogeing your time
ignoring other selves

Where did it all go?
Filched away
down some drain?
Was it spent
on some idle thrift?
Or on dreaming of a life
unlived, adrift
regretting and regretting
like a two faced Janus
forward and back
what might have beens

and the lack?

now is your reckoning
for your stolen time
– the weight of time
– the wait of time
time, that precious fleece
a lamb's coat
that Argo seeked at such a cost
sought, and found and lost
fleeced by the time you stole

Then, searching your own skin for scars
from work remembered
here a house built
and there a tree started
the hands that bore up that lowly
cruciform on which you worked
your ragged life
on which you were born
upon which you'll hang
bleating and waiting for slaughter
waiting for laughter

21st July 2018

The Folks Who Live Down the Road
– A love letter

I love you
Let's be clear
you are all to me
have no fear

My darling loves
My heart's core
My sweethearts
My neighbours next door

You've shaped my life
honed it to a tee
when I open my door
there you are – for me

You've never left me
constant, and I
will never
never say bye-bye

You smile when
we pass
I cheer your lives
I am your ass

Now leaves yonder

are browning in autumn's hue
but still you rumble by
as constant as your tattoos

Soon winter's comfort
will fill my days
with your revulsion
and poisoned hearsay

I love you
and your passing slights
keep grinning
you killed me, you shites

I would tell you
but I know not how
Love's hate
can bring one so low

If I could kill that love
that hate I would you know
for a penny fee
with just one blow

Yet here I remain
and you'll never know
how I died
my lovers, my beaux

September 1st 2018

The Kind Mason

Cut my words deep
kindly mason
cut 'em deep.
For even in stone
They all too quickly fade
In my long long sleep

12th September 2018

The Second Tower

Between two huge towers
Leaning in like Pisas
Lie all the books of my life
From volumes long
to stories short
A pamphlet jammed there
An essay folded here
Ah yes, and some forgotten lines
now and then dogeared
marking time

All tell something
From right to left
And back
From youth's fruit
to aged pith
And Decrepit core
From slow growing
School's rote
to learned knowing

We quake and tremble
For what is beyond
That second tower
That looms as closer we get
Only peoms and short muses
Quicken to stuff the spaces now

Dark closes beneath
its ugly walls
Look back look back!
To the starting light
Now a distant glow
But the light excuses itself
And the library grows dim
Hushed silence the only sound

21st September 2018

I was literally laughing
(on putting out the Thursday rubbish)

Struggling with the detritus
black sack
clear sack
I happened upon une jeune femme
passing by

On her phone she squeezed
her way along Cramp Boulevard
    And to my delight spoke
    Not to me, but to her hand
    'Yeah? So, like, I was literally laughing. Yeah?'

I wondered how
after willing of the fatted calves
to perform in tandem
she could drag such a profound
expression of manifest idle thought
so succinctly
from such a quotidian mouth

Is it possible, I thought,
that laughter could be *illiterate*?
Reflecting on her passing,
yes, I concluded.
Relieved, I nestled
The sacks to await their collection
More Rubbish, more rubbish
from up and down the Boulevard.

27th September 2018

Ryanair:

the queen of the skies
She taxies she stalls
Charges for all
Cancels and fails
And sometimes she flies

The queen is calling
Gate thirty-eight
Shuffle and crush
You Push and you rush
But for God's sake don't be late

I am on a refugee boat
full to the brim
High above the sea
Trying to float
Trying to swim

Scratch cards prance
Down the aisles
Selling the dream
Leave me alone
I am in denial

Life vest under my seat
I reach down and touch it
A vest that means life
Perhaps I should don it

It sounds pretty neat

Landing ready to claim
Baggage and asylum
Take me away
Lock me away
But never let me back
To the queen of the skies

15th October 2018

The Control Tower

On the very far side
Across a fat runway
There squats an old
Control tower
Abandoned after losing control

Around are the bones
Of aircraft long dead
Scattered and flightless
Extinct rudderless
Naked waiting
for the breakers torch

The tower watches
Over them to the
Jets Easying in and out
As Pigeon Passengers
preen and peck and coo
Follow the rules,
The lines, the calls
The breadcrumb trails
Controlled
they Ready themselves
for flight
kid themselves
This is their pigeon freedom

It squats in the encroaching trees
Watching dumbly
Of another time
when to fly
Was to wonder
To let slip the surly
Bonds of earth

I just long to step
Back into that time
Through the creaking
half hanging doors
Up the grubby steps
and gaze out
Its grimy shattered lenses
To those silvered birds
lifting and roaring and soaring
To gently brush an unpainted sky

17th October 2018

Failure to relaunch

What a hoot
are all the times
I have tried to reboot
to just end up
where I started
by the same old route

30th October 2018

Gratuities

(Carol to be sung along to *There is a Green Hill Far Away)*

There is a food bank
just outside
donated by the EU
where sly Cameron
and smug Bojo
will never ever go

You cannot say
You cannot tell
you were not warned at all
yet here you are
out in the cold
and all of it foretold.

16 December 2018

On Responsibility

I am worried (of course)
about my blocked and running nose
running out of control
but believe it to be from my friend Enzo
I could be wrong
What ever it is
or what it becomes
is nothing to do with me
but it is of me.
I did not wish it
do not want it
but it is me
And because it is me
I feel responsible
But it is responsibility without power
like the poor parents
whose children hunger
They do not wish it
do not want it
But poor is what they are
And I feel responsible
for the refugees
who from dangers run
They do not wish it
do not want it
But they are fearful
And I feel responsible
in the sun dappled glade

where a gin trapped fox
has gnawed herself free
she did not wish it
did not want it
still she is lame
and yet still I feel responsible
for the wordless poet
the colour blind painter
the writer blocked
the widow's loss
the junkie's arm
the warrior's tear
And always, always the lovers' shattered hearts

For all of this I somehow feel responsible

Does everyone feel this way?
Does everyone have an Enzo?
(For I am the prisoner of Enzo)
If not
I feel responsible

Do you?

20th January 2019

Well

There's a well
A deep well in our garden
Dug a while ago now
when the digging was good
and hope was kindled in its promise

The well digger knowing his craft
dowsed the ground and said
'here, we dig here' and
as the hole deepened
behind him the house rose
stone by stone in expectation
of the well diggers promise kept
'water will be found,'
He'd said
'go, build your house'

and, sure as his pledge
at the bottom of the shaft
a grimy face it's
teeth yellow in the candle's light
and two eyes shining up
contented and bright

to the tiny circle of friends
Water!
It bubbled and swirled
licked and rose
The first cup went to the first child
and she drank deep as the well

Well done, well dug, well digger!
they celebrated and
dressed the well with flowers and ribbons
and feted the digger-dowser
- in the custom

That ancient water is there
brooding – still
and I long to shout for my dreams
and call down my curses and wishes
to what may dwell there
and echo up a bucket of promises
filled full and fulfilled

23rd January 2019

They

They sleep
They sleep
They sleep to dream
And when they dream
They dream of sleep

25th February 2019

Tricks

I remember I used to think
her breasts were real.
It's strange the tricks
mammaries can play on you
and the way they make you feel.

13th March 2019

Questions

An old man bending
his ear
to a small boy
Asks
What will you do with all those years?

He thinks
then
looks at the old man
Whiskered in age
Furrowed with rage
At the turns
Of life's cruel page

The boy spoke
And asked almost in fun
Is there anything that is not
Possible?
That cannot be done?

The man straightens
And wants to tell him truth
Surveys his own life
Of promise and hope
Turned to mire and strife

His old eyes curtain with tears
That worry the boy
Then smiles
To Gentle his fears.

No, says the man
Not a one
Go, go and chase the sun
So no one will ask you
after all your years,
What did you do?
What was it you've done?

14/03/2019

Take the Low Road

Let us sit in the pub
And talk of kitchens
and bathrooms
and the death of things

Then when we are done,
Of holidays in the sun
Of money spent
And saved
On this and tat
It's so much fun

We'll brag softly
And shout loudly
Of how our lives
Are so sweet
Of what we own,
And have,
So proudly

Think not, say
not of things
Of the shackled mind
Of man and woman in chains
Let's have another
Drink boys
And forget we have brains.

23 April 2019

Unfinished Work

(Sisyphus smiled – To Albert C)

Between the Mountains of the rich
And The valleys of the poor
Sisyphus smiled

Cursed he climbed and shoved
Intimate with that pebble
He rested against it
Despite its urging
and so it absorbed him
His skin
his sweat
his blood

His arms trembled with pain
His feet slippered in gore
slipped against the weight
His shoulders bruised and cut
He heaved and shoved
as it slowly crunched its familiar rut
Worn and smoothed
by their conjoined history

as time passed
flowers emerged and grew
then shrunk back to earth
Trees leafed bore fruit
that scattered the ground in his path
birds sang joyful accompaniment
and rain washed him clean

Now an old man
ragged but unaged
by time
that marks the passing seasons
and foreshadowed him
The nights blew long and cold
and the days hot as the rock he pushed

Suffering all of this
Still he smiled and never succumbed
Knowing after his journey's work
to the top
His descent would be joyous
The climb worthy of his toil

Those below could see him
But could not help
Those above could see him
And would not help

Once atop he could see his path
And each time called to those below to take care
Lest they were crushed

by the boulder's bounding career
as it came to its rest to wait
at rock-bottom for him to arrive
and begin once more just
time enough for those below
to bathe his wounds
feed his spirit
And bless his soul
they clapped his back
and wished him well
each time.

And their children became fathers
mothers became grandmothers
and on.

And on down the generations.

While those above
seeing his pain
Laughed at his endless failure
Why did he not dive
release him from the mountain's grip?
Reaching the ground
Before his rock
No
Gravity's agent gives him time
To gaze about in glory

Camus' myth and call to life
comes to mind
that
No matter the strife
Self slaughter is for fools
with no burden
no purpose
who have no rock
and no cause to smile

14th-18th June 2019

Will there be trains?

The train pulls in
And pulls me in
and gently pulls out
A one way ticket
I wave my goodbyes
As the Small Stationary group
Becomes smaller
I see them bend in tears
In farewell
And go on
And go on

Between points
Over a rail
Signal at green
I am jogged along
Willing to go
The Journey of a life
Time
Over
Soon enough

We rock and roll
To a rhythm
Station to station
Beat to beat

Track to track
It's music
Sings from the
Turn-tabling wheels

Tunnel ahead
Whistles in tune
Into the dark
Into the long

long dark
Too dark
To see
I see
My Terminus

As then there right there
the train slows
Slowly melts around me
and silence surrounds me
A pinprick
A light at tunnels end
Then another
Another
a brother
And soon my vision swarms
With stars
And I am filled with light

I look back
The train's tail light
A red dwarf
Now
I am left to
swim in the glory

July 1-3 2019

This is the man

Who never
Hammered a nail
Made sail
Turned a screw
Who
Never sawed
through a board
Invented a word
Never
Built a boat
Ever milked a goat
ever
laid a brick
learned a trick
or two
who
never painted a hall
plastered a wall
or even wondered
at all
about much
grand or small
But a man who
thought of himself

as god's gift to man
never once had to wait
in line for his plate
or beg at the gate
of some rich estate
but had lots of women
and became - PM

3rd July 2019

En Passant

Day to day weaves
in and out
for a transient
on the planet
And like some
Vladimir or Estragon
frayed and shoeless
near the end
of the wait
of the road
Will I have something
at the gate
for my passing
to show?

18 August 2019

The Well Digger (Pt2)

I know what is down in the well
There, in it's mysterious ink
It's history unwritten
it lays still
and brooding
sulking
forbidden the sun.

In that deep
amongst the forgotten wishes,
the dropped coins of long ago hopes
paid for but not realised,
dwells the remnant of a man

He used to love the well
it's deep forbidding mystery
the imagined wheel that hoisted the water
the bucket that washed
children of their play
And slaked eager mouths
thirsty from the field's labour

He imagined the well digger,
saw his sweat as he laid stone -
down – yet contra to gravity's insisting
Then, as water welled around him
a shout to the straining heads circled above
Oui! Nous avons de l'eau!
Nous avons de l'eau!

And now he mingles with all
becoming its part
its history
returning not to dust
but to where he emerged
countless eons before
water
and like the ancients
face upward
he wonders at the small light
A single star in his firmament

2nd September 2019

Mute 'n't Jeff

Hello Jeffrey
   It's Jeff
What did he say?
Say's he's deaf
   No, it's Jeff!
Would you like tea?
Tea Jeffrey?
   No, coffee?
Like your tea nice and milky right?
   No. Black coffee.
Sugar, nice and sweet eh?
There you go Sweety.
   No Sugar, no tea!
I've stirred it in
Such a sweet tooth.
Hasn't he?
   Christ!
Biscuit?
   Yes
No? Sure Jeffrey?
   Yes I want one
Never mind
I'll turn up the TV
   NO!
Look, Cash in the Attic
I like that show
Me too
   Arrgh! Help me!

Help me-he he-he...
It's lovely to see him laughing
It is
Help me – please
If you need help
let us know.
All right?
Jeffrey?
Jeffrey?
He's deaf.
Must be awful.

2nd October 2019

The Cancelling Place

There is a place
a collecting point,
whose vastness stretches
from some inner eye
to a far off
imagined horizon
It is filled with prayer
Of voices mute and loud

It is a place of prayer
but
Not some humble chapel
or vainglorious temple
Nor a soaring cathedral
of gargoyled towers
and gilded saints
But still a place for prayer

Prayers angry
bidding
wanting
hoping
pleading
bargaining
questioning
Prayers that lift the soul

for some
and Damn those of others
All that fly from mouths and minds
to the gathering place

It sorts and shuffles the
prayer cards
Someone praying for help
or win on the ponies
A sick child's cure
Another's for their enemies to die
Prayers
on a soldiers dying lips
A chorus from a spiralling plane
Prayers of thanks
for a crop brought in
A ship safe home
to a roulette spin
Prayers of blind faith
From a hospital bed
and from the high crucifix

In that place they are aggregated
Hefted in the balance
weighed in the cancelling
good to bad
positive to negative
those that wish for help
and those which condemn
in spite

They all add to nothing
and in the balance
none
are answered
save but a few
and I pray
for your's
and for mine

25th October 2019

Clocks

The clocks went back today
I wish I could send them back
back a long way
rewind them all the way
to 10 years-old-o'clock
and of happier chimes
in the long long days
of Children's Summer Time

Oh Boy! That would be something.
Wouldn't it?

27th October 2019

Si medicina humanum possit loqui

(Decata Dr LuMo)

I

Imodeium apud cadessareran
Domperidone sequitur una
Me delectat Omeprazol
sed potius suavis prednisolone
Dexamethasone quod Cortisone
Docetaxel artificianti est
Zometa quod Zoledronic et in nomen

II

Candesartan cilexitil
Lorvax XL quod Indapamide
Adcal et simastivan
Lymphoedema nam omne tempus
Zoladex punctatis latus

III

Prostatus intus invisibiliter habitat
ut qui tollis peccata mundi
Radium Ducenti viginti tres
saecula saeculorum
Amen

XII Lulii 2020

Reilly

Hey Reilly. How you doing boy?

Ok. How's you?

Ehh. Not so good.

How bout a walk?

Ja think it'll help?

Always done it for me.

I like you Reilly. I really do.
You're the dog I never had
and never will have.

That sure is ruff.
Ruff!

Now stop that!
Come on let's go.

21 July 2020

The Orbital Shore

Spring frocks the land
With duds and floral contraband

The silence of nature wronged
emptied of buzz and song

The moths defeat
the butterflies retreat

The insects' ravaged demise
near gone, but for the lording of the flies

Yet, I hear the long chatter
of the yellow jack hammer

And, yonder way, we harken
to the chainsaw's harsh barking

June buggers fill soft air
With whispers of an engine's blare

The land is in full bloom
Alive with lorries' sonic boom

Far away I hear the crashing roar
on the ceaseless orbital shore

Suck of tyre on tar counterfeits
the licking surf and seas' conceit

How cheap the deal we bought
how costly the ruin we wrought

June 1st 2020

The LockDown Isle of GB

(apologies WBY again)

I will sit and stay now, and stay in GB LockDown
In a small house here of bricks and mortar made
No PPE will there be here, no sign of surgical gowns
I'll live alone in the quiet and be sore afraid

And I will have some peas there for nothing can I grow
Dropped from the van of Morrisons, or substitutes it will
bring
Where sleep is a welcome guest, and cricket's not on show
And evening's are as silent as a telephone's ring

I will sit, and stay now, for always day and night
As I hear the natter of passers-by to and fro
At the window I'll stand in the lowering twilight
And wait in isolation for an end of this island's farrago.

5th June 2020

IPMS

Good morning. How can I help?

Is that the pain management department?

It is. How can I help?
Well, I am in increasing pain.

Right. Well, you need a IPMS from us.
IPMS?

An integrated pain management strategy. An IPMS
And that is?

Well,
it's a blended regimen of pills;
massage;
special pillows and chair;
a shit-upon commode;
stair lift;
some home help;
respite for the Mrs;
a touch of RT here
a tad of K-Mo there;
more pills;
not forgetting lots of simpering
embarrassed smiles around you;
patronising tones;
maybe a priest if you want to pray;
A Rabbi if you need to er, rabbit. Heh heh!

That kind of thing.
But all specially tailored to you
and your needs.
That sounds like a real pain.

There you have it.
It is a pain.
We do the management
and you do the pain.
Not called an Integrated PMS for nothing.
Have nice day.

August 12th 2020

Rainbow Pills

I take these yellow pills
For the side effects of which
I take these red pills

And for the red pill's
side effects I take these
Blue ones

This rainbow cocktail
of blue, red
and yellow pills produces
from me
(As you'd predict)
a white secretion

Which why I took the yellow
pills in the first place

7th September 2020

Possessions

There is a closet
a cache
wherein lies my heart

In there, still
 - beat the dreams
I had

Sometimes
I raid it
for a whiff of happiness

But now the ancient lock sticks
its hinge stiff
the door heavy and fast

One day, too old
I shall find it
locked, its key lost

Yet, I shall beat
my hearts door
until it breaks

and beats no more.

9th September 2020

The Imagined Tree - Arenas del Rey, Andalusia, Spain May 3rd 2016 10:13.08

Printed in Great Britain
by Amazon